ISBN: 1-56288-089-6 Library of Congress Catalog Card Number: 91-9675
Printed in the United States of America (F1/10) 0 9 8 7 6 5 4 3 2

MY DAD'S O·K·A·Y

·A MUDPIE ™ ·STORY·
straight·to·you·from·
·KITT'NVILLE· BY
GUY GILCHRIST

MUDPIE

CHECKERBOARD ☆ PRESS ☆
NEW YORK ·NEW YORK

My name is Mudpie. This book is about me and my dad.

I like to help my dad with chores around the house.

When my dad painted the house he let me help.
My dad's okay.

My dad painted the house.
I painted my dad.

When it's time to rake leaves, my dad lets me help. I'm not so good at raking.

 I'm much better at playing!

I climb the trees in my backyard and play king of the jungle. I look for lions and tigers and elephants.

Sometimes I climb so
high the ground gets
very far away.

That's when my dad rescues me!
My dad's okay.

One day I wanted to surprise my dad, so I washed his
car all by myself.

Boy! Was he ever surprised!

My dad and I play baseball. I am always the batter and
he is the pitcher. When I get a hit, we both make RAHHH
sounds. Just like the crowd is going crazy!
My dad's okay.

In the wintertime when it snows, we build
a snowman together. My dad always lets me
make the face.

At bedtime my dad makes me take a bath—even when I'm
not dirty. And he makes me brush my teeth, though I already
brushed them in the morning.
But my dad's okay.

He always hugs me good night and says, "I love you, Mudpie."